PON

Dear Parent:

Congratulations! Your child is taking the first steps on an exciting journey. The destination? Independent reading!

STEP INTO READING® will help your child get there. The program offers books at five levels that accompany children from their first attempts at reading to reading success. Each step includes fun stories, fiction and nonfiction, and colorful art. There are also Step into Reading Sticker Books, Step into Reading Math Readers, and Step into Reading Phonics Readers— a complete literacy program with something to interest every child.

Learning to Read, Step by Step!

Ready to Read   Preschool–Kindergarten
• big type and easy words • rhyme and rhythm • picture clues
For children who know the alphabet and are eager to begin reading.

Reading with Help   Preschool–Grade 1
• basic vocabulary • short sentences • simple stories
For children who recognize familiar words and sound out new words with help.

Reading on Your Own   Grades 1–3
• engaging characters • easy-to-follow plots • popular topics
For children who are ready to read on their own.

Reading Paragraphs   Grades 2–3
• challenging vocabulary • short paragraphs • exciting stories
For newly independent readers who read simple sentences with confidence.

Ready for Chapters   Grades 2–4
• chapters • longer paragraphs • full-color art
For children who want to take the plunge into chapter books but still like colorful pictures.

STEP INTO READING® is designed to give every child a successful reading experience. The grade levels are only guides. Children can progress through the steps at their own speed, developing confidence in their reading, no matter what their grade.

Remember, a lifetime love of reading starts with a single step!

For Molly.
Thank you for laughing at my bedtime stories
and helping me to make up Pinky Dinky Doo.

Special thanks to Katonah Elementary School

Photography by Sandra Kress

Digital coloring and compositing by Alisa Klayman-Grodsky

www.stepintoreading.com

Educators and librarians, for a variety of teaching tools, visit us at
www.randomhouse.com/teachers

Library of Congress Cataloging-in-Publication Data
Jinkins, Jim.
Pinky Dinky Doo : Where are my shoes? / by Jim Jinkins.
    p. cm. — (Step into reading. A step 3 book)
SUMMARY: Pinky Dinky Doo, an imaginative young girl, tells her brother and her pet guinea pig a silly story about a mixed-up day when everyone wore food for shoes.
ISBN 0-375-82914-8 (trade) — ISBN 0-375-92712-3 (lib. bdg.) — ISBN 0-375-82712-9 (pbk.)
[1. Shoes—Fiction. 2. Food—Fiction. 3. Imagination—Fiction.
4. Brothers and sisters—Fiction. 5. Storytelling—Fiction.]
I. Title. II. Series: Step into reading. Step 3 book.
PZ7.J57526Pi 2004 [E]—dc21 2003004026

Printed in the United States of America First Edition 10 9 8 7 6 5 4 3 2 1

Pinky Dinky Doo™

WHERE ARE MY SHOES?

by Jim Jinkins

Random House New York

Mommy Doo

Daddy Doo

Mr. Guinea Pig

Tyler Doo

Pinky Dinky Doo

Daffinee Toilette

Nicholas Biscuit

Bobby Boom

"Okay, Tyler!

I'm going to make up a story about

a girl named Pinky Dinky Doo!"

"Hey! That's your name!"

Tyler shouted.

"Exactly!" Pinky Dinky said.

"You just scored a Pinky Dinky Do!"

"All right!" Tyler yelled.

"I'll just shut my eyes,

wiggle my ears,

and crank up my imagination,"

said Pinky.

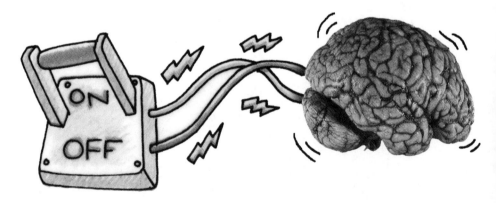

"The name of this story is . . ."

WHERE ARE MY SHOES?

A made-up story
by Pinky Dinky Doo

Cool
name.

It was a brand-new day in

Great Big City.

Pinky Dinky Doo woke up,

just like always.

Mr. Guinea Pig, the guinea pig,

gave Pinky Dinky Doo a big,

sloppy good-morning kiss.

Pinky jumped out of bed.

She went to the bathroom

and washed her . . .

 Pet guinea pig, Mr. Guinea Pig

 Monster truck,

the Pinky Dinky Dozer

C Face

That's easy!

It's  !

Pinky Dinky Doo washed her face,
of course!

After that, she put on a freshly ironed . . .

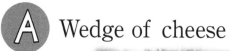 Wedge of cheese

B Pony

C Dress

Don't be silly! Pinky Dinky Doo didn't put on a pony or a wedge of cheese!

"The answer is **C**.

She put on a dress," said Pinky.

Downstairs, Pinky ate
a great big bowl of
Frosted Brainiac Flakes.

"Hurry up,
Pinky Dinky,
or you'll be late
for school,"
Mommy Doo
called.

Pinky Dinky Doo ran upstairs
to finish getting ready.

But to her surprise,
she couldn't find her shoes!!

Pinky Dinky Doo looked
under her bed.

No shoes.

Pinky
did some
deep-closet
diving.

No
shoes!

She even looked in the potty,
just in case Tyler, her brother,
had put them there.

No such luck.

This is definitely a
Pinky Dinky Don't!

Beep! Beep! Beep!

"Oh no!" Pinky said.

"There's the school bus!"

Pinky Dinky didn't know what to do!

"I can't go barefoot," she said.

Pinky Dinky ran from room to room looking for ideas. She put two comfy chairs on her feet. But they were not comfy.

She tried two canoes. But she couldn't find the paddles.

Pinky even put on a pair of clocks. But she was running out of time.

Get it?

"Pinky!"

Mommy Doo shouted.

"Bus! Leave! School! Now!!!"

Pinky was getting exasperated!

Pinky Dinky Doo zoomed

to the kitchen.

She grabbed her

double baloney sandwich and

out of the clear blue sky,

Pinky got an idea!

She opened the sandwich and pulled
out the two pieces of baloney.

Then she wrapped them
around her feet
and used string beans
to hold them in place.

Yum,
baloney.

And off Pinky went.

Bye, Mom! Love you!

Mommy Doo sighed.
"Did my daughter
just get on the bus
wearing baloney
for shoes?"

At school, Pinky Dinky Doo saw
her best friend, Nicholas Biscuit.

Pinky

She told him about
her missing shoes.
"I don't believe it,"
Nicholas shouted.

"Look!"
His feet were
smashed into
two meat loaves.

Meat
loafers

Ketchup
socks

RING!

Just then the bell rang.
It was time for class!

"Come on, Nicholas," Pinky said.

Pinky Dinky Doo and Nicholas

snuck into class.

They hoped no one would see

their crazy shoes.

Their teacher, Ms. Maganza,
was telling the class a true story.
A funny thing happened that day.

"I couldn't find my shoes," she said.
"So I had to wear two roasted chickens!"
Luckily, she had a third chicken
she could use as a purse.
It matched her shoes perfectly.

Instantly, the class was buzzing.
All the kids said they couldn't find
their shoes, either.
Abby B. had wrapped
spaghetti around her feet
to make ballet slippers.

Meatball tutu

Bobby Boom had on
feet-filled doughnuts.

Daffinee Toilette was
wearing melons.

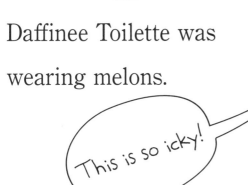

This is so icky!

Everybody was talking and laughing and showing off their food shoes.
Then Ms. Maganza turned on the TV.

"Attention, all teachers and students! This is Principal Dipthong."

"Due to a mix-up in our school kitchen, today's lunch will be . . .

Slipper Salad

Barbecued
Cowboy Boots

And for dessert . . .

Frozen Flip-Flops."

"Gross!"

Daffinee squealed.

"Whoever heard of

shoes for lunch?"

"What are we going

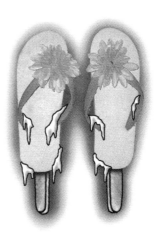

to do for food?" Bobby moaned.

Pinky Dinky decided to Think Big!

"Stand back!" Nicholas shouted.

Everybody made room

for Pinky to use her brain.

Normally, it was an

everyday, kid-sized brain . . .

until she started to think big!

She thought and thought and thought!

And as she thought,

her brain got bigger and bigger

until her head filled the room.

And then it happened . . .

Pinky Dinky Doo had a big idea.

"She's gonna blow!" Nicholas shouted. The pressure from all that thinking shot out of Pinky's ears. She flew around the room like a balloon losing air.

"Hey! I know what we can do!" Pinky said. "Why don't we . . .

A Sit in the corner and drool like baboons?

B Cry like babies with gas?

C Eat our food shoes and wear our shoe food?"

Pinky answered her own question.

"It's  C , of course," she said.

"Come on, let's eat our shoes!"

Everyone cheered Pinky's good idea.

"Hurray for Pinky Dinky Doo!"

they shouted.

Then they all trooped down
to the cafeteria.
Pinky led the way.

First, all the kids sorted through the cafeteria dishes to match up the pairs of shoes.

Can you help everyone
find their missing shoes?

Then they put their food shoes
on the table.

It was a feast of meat loaf,

melon, doughnuts, chicken,

spaghetti, and baloney.

They ate and ate and ate and ate.

It was the best school lunch ever.

"And that's *exactly* what happened.
Sort of," Pinky said to Tyler.
"The end."

Tyler looked worried.

Pinky knew what he was thinking.

"P.S. And since this was a made-up
story, you don't have to worry
about dirty food or germs or
STINKY FEET!" Pinky added.

Tyler was relieved.

"I loved that story!" Tyler yelled.

"Thanks, Tyler," said Pinky.

"Which part did you like best?"

"Uh . . . um . . . I forgot," said Tyler.

"Well," asked Pinky, "did you like
the girl named Pinky Dinky Stinky?"

"No!" Tyler shouted.

"Her name is Pinky Dinky *Doo!*"

"How about when Pinky got a big, sloppy kiss from Mr. Guinea Pig, the musk ox?" Pinky asked.
"No!" Tyler said.

"Mr. Guinea Pig is a guinea pig!" Mr. Guinea Pig made a funny face.

"Did you like it when Pinky couldn't find her brain?" Pinky asked.

"No!" Tyler shouted.

"It was her shoes! She couldn't find her shoes!"

"Wow, Tyler, you remembered
my story really well!" Pinky said.

"Pinky," Tyler asked, "do you think
I'll ever be able to make up stories
as good as yours?"

"Sure!" Pinky said.

"I bet *you* can make up a story, too!"